Chapter 1: A Hunting We Will Go

As "A hunting we will go, a hunting we will go, hi ho the derry-o, a hunting we will go" runs through my head maniacally, I can't stop to wonder if this will be the time I get caught. It is always a possibility, no matter how remote. However, I think I would like to feel the roughness of their hands on me as they force me down onto the unyielding cement. The way the cold steel would wrap around my wrists tightly as their bodies weigh heavily on me and won't let me move an inch.

There is just something about how a man gets excited when he can unleash his aggressive side that turns me on endlessly. When Jon does, I can't get enough, even if it is from the sidelines for the most part while she is on the receiving end of it. Of course, maybe that is why I get off so easily when she experiences pain, because I want her to feel what I have endeared for her all those years in her place.

When I turn around and spot the perfect mark, I stop as a man in his 30's wearing a very expensive looking tailored dark grey pinstripe suit, and a gold Rolex sits down across from me at the bar. I swallow hard and then put on my best most seductive smile as I uncross my legs and run my fingertips up the sensitive skin there. He watches as the hem of my black silk dress rises and he catches a glimpse of my swollen folds, if only for an instant as I giggle and quickly release the fabric so no one else can see.

His hand instantly seeks out the heat between my legs as he licks his lips and then states rather insistently with a deep, hoarse voice, "You will never forget what I am about to do to you, I can promise you that."

Because I am playing the game, I stare deep into his eyes and then laugh as I smack at his hand playfully. His fingers slide up even further so I spread them just an inch so he can gain access while I smirk with delight. He leans forward and as the tip of his index finger brushes my slit, he whispers in my ear, "I want to taste your sweetness before I bury my cock so deep in you that it hurts."

As I watch him bring his finger to his lips, a look of complete pleasure crosses his face and then he whispers breathlessly, "You are sinfully delicious. I must have more now."

The moment he takes my hand and leads me out to his Hummer, I start to feel the irresistible pull of my blade as it sits in the bottom of my purse calling to me. Feed me, I need to feel the blood as it sprays all over my hilt. I want to feel warm again.

"I have a better idea." I say seductively as I pull him towards my car.

"Let's go back to my place." I purr softly as I wink at him suggestively.

"Mm. Sounds lovely." He replies quickly but then looks back to the Hummer and asks hesitantly, "But what of my ride?"

I smirk while shaking my head slowly and then I say absentmindedly, "It will be fine until we get back. Besides, I know you want to do more than just fuck in the back of your car." I pause before adding wickedly, "Sometimes these things can take hours if not days and if you tie me down, you can do anything you want to me. I mean anything."

As soon as I say it, I see the glint flicker in his dark brown eyes while he smiles from ear to ear. Then he flicks his tongue out and licks his chops like a wolf hungrily watching his prey.

"There is a thing or two I wouldn't mind doing to you." He whispers quietly as he leans in within an inch of my face, and I feel the warmth of his breath as it moves my hair across my cheek.

"Good, because I get a kick out of being dominated and I absolutely love pain." I say slowly as every word drips with seductiveness.

When he flicks his tongue out again and licks my cheek, it takes me by surprise and weirds me out in a strange sort of way. I feel as if he is tasting his next meal. In all honesty, to be on the receiving end of this game is out of the ordinary for me. So, I cock my head and run my finger down his rock-hard abdomen before I stop at his swollen shaft.

His eyes light up and he groans when I wrap my fingers around his balls. "Fuck, you know how to handle a man, don't you?" he says quietly while looking at the two men's faces highlighted in neon who just walked out the front doors of the bar.

The sign that says Dave's is lit up in neon lights, so it is easily seen from the road for at least a half a mile each way.

"Come on let's go before we draw any unwanted attention." He says suggestively when he notices that the two men are quickly walking our way.

"Hey, buddy. How about we take your watch and that woman on your arm? I bet we could use both." The taller man with the tenor voice yells as he pulls out his switchblade from his faded jeans.

The other man pulls a pistol out of his waist band and stares at me hungrily while not saying a thing. I clear my throat and then watch as they both rush the gentleman whom I was going to have some fun with, or not. At this moment, I might as well just go home because these two have just squashed my fun for the night. However, I may still be able to salvage it.

As the shorter man with the gun thrusts the tip into my side, I back hand him and he turns to look at me wildly. I stare up into his eyes and dare him loudly, "Why don't you try that again mother fucker? This time do it like a real man without the gun in my side."

I feel his nails dig into the skin of my arm as he spins me around and continues to look at me wildly as he threatens, "Cunt! Who the fuck do you think you are? I am about to blow your fucking head off after I fuck you six ways from Sunday."

I start to laugh because right now this is as funny as it gets. I roll my eyes and then reply as I spit in his face vehemently, "Can you say fuck a couple more times?"

A second later, I watch as the taller man shoves the businessman down to his knees violently after he takes his Rolex and his wallet. Then he looks over to where we are standing as he asks flatly, "What's the plan Dan?"

"Damnit! I fucking told you to never say my name!" he exclaims loudly as he jerks me around and tightens his grip on me while flailing the gun around in their general direction.

I am not surprised at all when his finger slips on the trigger and the gun goes off as loud as a firework. A puff of gun powder floats through the air as the bullet rips through the taller man's head. And when the shock of what he has done hits Dan, he drops the gun to the ground as he stares at the taller man's dead body.

A few minutes later when the sirens start to blare in the distance, he finally releases me before he runs off into the darkness. I, on the other hand, decided that I must disappear before the cops get here for an entirely different reason.

"Come on, let's get out of here before they arrive." I yell at the man in the suit covered in the taller man's blood.

For one thing I still can salvage what I started. The other, if I let him get caught by the cops, he might mention that he was about to go off with me. I can't ever let that happen, even if I secretly want to get caught.

After he shakes his head several times, he stands up and tries to wipe the blood off his face as we run towards my car. I unlock it quickly and we both climb inside just before the cops pull in the parking lot. While scanning the area, I see the back entrance and silently slip out before anyone notices us.

"Thank goodness." I think to myself as I slide down in the seat and relax for the moment, because now I can continue with my plan.

Chapter 2: Timing Is Everything

"I simply can't believe that I made it out of there by the seat of my pants." I say absentmindedly as I open the door to my spare apartment on 43rd street.

"Tell me about it." The man in the suit utters under his breath as he looks me up and down slowly with wicked intent.

Just as soon as we make it inside and I shut the door, he slams me up against it and shows me how strong he really is. While wedging me between his muscular body and the dark oak door, I begin to feel my heightened senses go into overdrive. Not only do I suddenly smell his overly expensive French cologne hit me like a brick, but I watch as perspiration forms on the skin of his neck.

When the vein begins to throb on his forehead, it reminds me of why we are here. I need to kill before Jon finds that I am not there. And the sheer fact that time is running out does not escape me. Instead, I expedite this whole thing so I can wrap it up quickly by smirking and then saying huskily as he stares at me hungrily, "Is that all?"

He throws his head back and laughs loudly. Then he returns his gaze to mine and claims my mouth forcefully while he holds my hands above my head and tightens his grip on my wrists so much that it hurts. "Ah, the pain….." I think to myself with satisfaction when my nipples become hard, and my folds start to throb in need.

It is precisely at this moment that I hear my phone start to ding. I furrow my brow and turn my head sharply to the side to break the kiss quickly because I realize that it must be Jon. Damn him. Of all people, why did he have to text me right at this moment? When I was about to get my satisfaction.

"Fuck!" I cry out before he releases my hands and backs up with a curious look in his eyes.

By the time I reach the phone in my purse, it already begins ringing.

"Is that your husband?" he asks slyly before I see a smirk form in the corners of his lips.

"No. Just a boy toy." I reply softly before raising my finger to my lips and hushing him while I hit the answer button.

His smirk turns slowly to a Cheshire Cat smile as his hands return to my body. At first his palms roam over my hips slowly in appreciation, but then he lowers them to the hem of my outfit. As his fingers trail underneath and up the sensitive skin of my inner thighs, a soft moan escapes my lips and I close my eyes to shut him out temporarily.

"Hey, where are you?" Jon asks impatiently at the other end of the phone as I hear his hoarse voice become angry.

For a moment there is silence as I think of what to say and then when I feel fingers rubbing my slit gingerly, I swallow hard and blurt out, "Jon, not now. I am busy. I had to go visit my girlfriend Rosey out of the city. Just shortly after you left, she called and told me she needed me. A guy had just tried to rape her on her way home from the gym and she didn't know what to do so she tazed him. However, it seems that it didn't last long enough because he has followed her home. As a matter of fact, I am looking out the window and I can see his car with him sitting in the driver's seat, staring at her front door."

"Well, tell her I am sorry, but I had thought we agreed that you would be here when I returned. I need to have a talk with you, and it is of the utmost importance that I do it now before I chicken out." He says in a matter-of-fact tone of voice, after sighing heavily.

I swallow hard as I feel his middle finger slip in just an inch. As he does it, his smile disappears as he reaches around to my rear with his other hand, and he stares at me with a glint in his eyes. When he trails down my crack with his fingers, I already know what he is going to do, so I smirk and wait for it.

"Give me an hour and I will be there. I need to console her and wait until the cops show up before I leave her alone." I say hesitantly after sighing heavily.

I get the feeling that we both know it is a lie, but he gives in reluctantly and replies sternly, "Alright, but no more than that because you need to follow the rules."

"Fine." I answer quickly as a manicured nail traces my rim and then slides in.

As soon as I hit the end button, I drop the phone to the floor and run a hand into his hair before grasping a handful and tugging on it, so he is forced to kiss me hard on the lips. I bite his lower lip playfully after he comes up for air and then he stuffs two more fingers in each hole. God, I love this man and I have barely met him, but only for a quick fuck and then to slit his throat. After all, I am compelled to feel that warmth between my legs and then on my blade because it keeps calling to me.

When I break the kiss this time by shoving him backwards forcefully, I growl needfully, "I need you to fuck me now. I only have a few minutes, so use it well."

He smirks and then slips his fingers out before sliding his hands up to my waist and then hoisting me over his shoulder. While he carries me down the hallway, I yell, "The last room on the right."

He seems to understand because a minute later, he kicks the door open violently and then throws me down on the bed before commanding and pointing, "Get down on all fours. I want to fuck your ass like you have never been before. I sure hope you are ready for this one."

I do as he says, but before I brace myself, I turn my head and watch as he whips out the biggest monster dick I have ever seen. Apparently, I misjudged him and almost missed out on the ride of my life.

"Baby, he wants to make you bleed." He says breathlessly as he begins to stroke him with both hands slowly while looking at my dripping pussy.

"Actually, I have a better idea first." He adds a moment later when he twirls his finger around in gesture for me to turn around and face him.

With mouth open, and big round eyes, I swallow hard because I don't know if I can even get that horse cock inside of my mouth.

"You are going to choke on him and just before you black out, I will slide him out and then fuck every orifice until I cum everywhere. Baby, you won't know what's happening by the time I get through with you. Matter of fact, you won't be going home tonight to that loser, I have other plans for that luscious body of yours." He says gruffly before rubbing the tip on my lips.

"That's a girl. You are such a good girl that I know you can swallow him." He says while coaxing me to open wide as he forcefully shoves him in. "I know you can do it baby girl. Open that throat for me nice and wide." He commands me as I start to choke.

It is a strange feeling, choking on a man's huge donkey dick. Knowing that he has the power over you and can kill you if he keeps going, makes my pussy throb even more.

"Oh, fuck that feels good." He cries out as I tighten my throat and mouth around his rock-hard shaft while he thrusts it in and out slowly.

It pulsates and throbs to the beat of my ever-growing need. And if he doesn't fill the void quickly, I may need to end this all prematurely because my vision is starting to fade. Everything starts to go dark as I continue to choke on him, and he fucks my throat more and more forcefully.

Chapter 3: In Trouble

I wake up to a sore throat and the feeling that I have been in this situation before as I am being filled in both holes and spread eagle on my stomach. As he grunts and moans loudly, I discover that my arms and legs are tied tightly with heavy duty rope after I turn my head enough to look down and see that I am literally fucked. So, I try to get free, but it is no use because he has all the power now and I can't do anything about it. I do not even know how long I have been out. But what I do know is that I am his now to do whatever he wants with. For all I know, he could be a serial killer as well, or a rapist and I walked right into his trap, not the opposite.

When I start to laugh maniacally, the constant thrusting between my legs stops as he pauses and asks curiously while cocking his head, "What's so funny? I surely would have thought you would have started crying or screaming by now as soon as you realized that you are in danger."

After swallowing hard, I reply proudly, "Oh, hell no. I love it. This is going to make me cum so hard."

The Cheshire Cat smile returns to his handsome face now as I notice the rest of his clothes are gone. When my eyes move down, I watch as his muscles twitch and flex. "Boy, at least if I am going to go out this way, it will be by someone who has a huge dick!" I think to myself and laugh.

As I continue to stare at his body, I wonder if he shaves his chest because it is as smooth as a baby's butt. His skin glistens in the light of the room almost as if he oils it. How ironic that someone so pretty has the balls to do this to me?

I laugh out loud again and then roll my eyes as he digs his nails into my hips and fucks me harder than he had been previously. He raises his hand before smacking my ass so hard that I wince, and then he slides a big black vibrator in and out of my ass slowly. It feels so good that when I cum no more than a minute later, it hits me like a thunderous lightning clap as I begin to shake from head to toe. When I clench down on his cock, he stops suddenly and yells before thrusting through it, "That's it my good girl. You are so tight, and I am afraid that I have made you bleed, but now you are just the right size for me everywhere. I think we will get along famously my sweet little thing."

I close my eyes just in time to feel my soaked, bleeding folds, get filled to the brim with hot spurts of his seed. He sighs and then leans down to whisper in my ear, "Fuck, I love the way you feel and when I make you have my baby, I will love that too. Matter of fact, if it is a girl, I think I will call her Babygirl as well when she is old enough."

At that moment, I snap when I hear him say it and suddenly, I am all eyes on a way of getting out of here. However, a second later, I do not expect his body to jerk back and get thrown clear across the room. "Fuck, who the hell are you? I was just joking around." He yells angrily before Jon's fist connects with his jaw and he cries out in pain as I hear a bone shattering crunch.

When Jon reaches down with both hands and twists the man's neck effortlessly, I can already tell by the popping sound, that he has just killed him. I stare at him as Joanna leaves me now that I am safe and I ask hesitantly in curiosity, "How the hell?"

He smirks and then stands up before walking over to where I am tied up. And when he reaches me, he stops and cocks his head before answering, "Christy, I put a tracker on your phone number. There is an app that can track anyone if you know their number."

"What?" I ask hesitantly while acting stupid, even though I already know about it.

While rolling his eyes, he pretends he doesn't hear me and begins to untie the ropes that are tightly wrapped around my wrists, then the ones on my ankles. When he is finished, I sit up and rub my left hand because it is raw and bleeding from me trying to get out of my restraints the moment I woke up. As I look up into his handsome face, he stares back at me worriedly and then asks in a whisper after an uncomfortably long silence, "Why? I thought we had something special."

I swallow hard again as I realize what Joanna did was wrong, but it is too late now. So, I reply sarcastically, "Well, I guess you shouldn't have left me alone."

He shakes his head back and forth slowly with his eyes shut and then he reopens them before answering hurtfully, "I guess not. I thought I could trust you because I see that you keep a knife under your pillow, but you haven't used it on me yet."

I quickly turn away and stare at the wall, because if he knows about my knife, maybe he knows about my past time as well. How could he though? Unless…. "You are an idiot! He is a cop."

I shake my head in frustration and refuse to believe it. After all, he did just kill a man. If he is a cop, he couldn't do that. Could he? After all, he must follow the laws just like everyone else does or he goes to prison too.

"Jon, there is so much that you don't know about me. And honestly, I am afraid to tell you because you will run out the door and never look back if you knew. I have had too hard of a life for this and now I am afraid that I will lose you." I say unwillingly because my heart won't be able to take this break if that is what this is.

"So be it. You have seen me now at my most vulnerable. So, if you decide to leave, I will completely understand once I confide in you. When I tell you this, you will find it hard to believe and will probably walk right out that door and never look back. I won't blame you if you do. But don't judge me because you have no idea what I have been through." I murmur softly as I limp around the room and struggle to find my clothes.

When I feel his warm hand on mine, I lean on him, and we find them together. As I get dressed, I sit down carefully on the edge of the old wooden bed and stare at him as he kneels in front of me while helping me. He gazes into my eyes afterwards and we say nothing for several long minutes, until he asks, "So, what could possibly be so horrible that I would go running the moment you told me?"

I hesitate and then the words rush out as if the flood gates had been opened, because finally, I could tell someone who cares enough about me to ask, "When I was a little girl, my dad molested me. Not once, but over many years until I finally did something about it. What is worse, is the fact that I have a split personality. Please don't hate me." I pause as the tears cascade down my cheeks and his big hands brush them away so sweetly.

He leans over and kisses the rest of them away before he stops me from going on. "I don't need to know any more now. What I do need to do is drive you home and take care of you. Hush and let me do this." He says in almost a whisper as his lips brush over mine so softly and filled with love.

After he scoops me up in his arms and he carries me to his car, I wait as he takes care of the body by rolling it up in the bedroom carpet and then throwing it into the trunk. As soon as he sits down and shuts the door, I turn to him and ask hesitantly, "What are you going to do with him?"

"Just don't you worry about it. I have a special place just for this sort of thing." He whispers as the look on his face tells it all.

He has done this before, and I don't know why I am not the least bit surprised.

Chapter 4: Jon's Real Life

When I back out of the asshole's driveway carefully, I look both ways through the blinding sunlight, and then speed down the road as quickly as possible so no one sees us leaving. I have already jeopardized everything by the way I handled this. However, there was no other way around it and when I turn to face her briefly a few minutes later, I notice that she is staring out the window silently.

Before I say anything, I swallow hard and then run my right hand over my forehead to brush the sweat from my brow, while I think about everything that has happened so far. To say the least, there is no way that I can report this to the captain now. I would be a fool if I tried and would end up in jail instead.

"Christy, I still don't see why I would run away from that. You have done nothing wrong except for the fact that you should have stayed where I told you to. You knew that I would be back soon. But then you not only lied to me about being at a girlfriend's house, but you fucked someone else when I thought we were starting to have feelings for each other. Am I wrong?" I say softly at first but then start to feel angrier every second I keep going.

As I slam my fist down on the steering wheel, I glance back at her and catch her staring right at me with contempt in her eyes. Something I didn't think I would see, but there it is as plain as day and now she is glaring at me as well.

"What?" I scream while running my hand through the back of my hair and then blow air out in a huff.

She sits there quietly while wringing her fingers in her lap and then she finally speaks in a whisper while simultaneously snapping at me, "You surprise me. One moment you act like the night in shining armor. The next you are quite the prick!"

I whip my head around and ask angrily, "Excuse me? What is your problem? I just saved your life, and this is the thanks I get. Let me stop the car and let your highness out right here. By the way, don't let the door hit you in the ass on the way out!" I exclaim loudly while pulling over to the side of the road as I apply the brake and scowl at her.

Just as soon as the car has stopped, I watch as she flings her door open wildly and climbs out. She sighs softly and then turns to frown at me before replying sadly, "I knew you were too good to be true."

I sit there and stare after her for a moment until I get so mad that I slam both of my fists down on the steering wheel and then exclaim violently, "Fuck!"

How could this have happened? More importantly, how did this whole thing with her happen in the first place? It was supposed to be just a job, not a big mistake. Now I might have to find a way of making her disappear too because I can't have her running around and telling people that I just killed some moron.

Even though no one would believe it, I can't chance anyone looking into my extra-curricular activities. Because then, I would have some know it all detective hunting me down, just like when I was appointed to her case.

While shaking my head, I slam my fists down again and then yell, "Fuck it.

Christy, get back here." As I watch her disappear over the hill.

When I can't believe that I am letting a woman get this far under my skin, I quickly reach over and shut the passenger side door before putting the car back into gear and speeding after her. "Fuck, fuck, fuck, fuuuuuuck!" I exclaim one last time as she comes into view when I drive over the hill and slow down quickly.

I narrowly escape hitting her because she has stopped right in the middle of the road and is just staring at me. Is she trying to get hit? Or is she testing me? This woman has bigger balls than most of the men I know.

After staring her down, I lean out the window and yell, "Christy, get your ass over here and get in. We need to talk, now."

She continues to glare at me and then finally after I open my door and act like I am about to get out, she walks towards the car quickly. While saying nothing, she opens the door before sitting down and then stares blankly at me.

"Shut the door." I say forcefully as I point in its general direction.

She stares at me for a few more seconds before she finally does and then I watch as she buckles herself in. Once she glances back at me, I put the car into gear, and we head towards the lake silently. Neither one of us says anything until we reach the dirt road off the highway.

As soon as we do, she turns to look at me with wide eyes and asks hesitantly, "Is this where we are dumping the body?"

I sigh before I reply slowly, "Yes, this is my special spot. No one else knows about it and I have never taken another soul here before, literally."

She cocks her head curiously and stares at me for a moment as if in deep thought before she asks slowly while tapping her perfectly manicured nails on the door handle, "So, how many people have you killed?"

Why would she ask me this unless she truly gets me? So, after I sit and mull it over and over in my head while gazing at her appreciatively, I finally realize one thing. I must tell her and gauge her reaction.

"Alright, I will confide in you only if you tell me how you got rid of your parents." I reply sarcastically as a smile spreads across my lips.

Chapter 5: Truths

After he pulls over onto the soft shoulder and puts the car into park, he gazes at me as I fidget in my seat. Because I start to feel self-conscious, I stare down at my hands before I say in a hushed, slow voice, "The last time my dad decided to molest me, I stopped him right as he began to take his pants down. I didn't give him more than a second to think about what I was doing before I walked up behind him and slit his throat without a moment of hesitation. As soon as I felt the warmth of the blood on my hands, I knew that I was a natural born killer and from that time on I haven't been able to escape the call of the kill. It calls to me in the most inconvenient times. When it does, I hear this voice as clear as day, beckoning me to feel the blood as it gushes from my victim's veins. What bugs me the most is that until now, the only way I could ever get off was knowing that I was about to kill him after I felt the rush of an orgasm."

I pause before glancing over at his face and noticing the calm look on it. It is not one of shock but knowing. Are we one in the same? What is the likelihood that I would chance upon someone so much like me and that we are more than compatible. Maybe even meant to be. Even though Joanna is the one who takes over, I have always known that I was the one who was ultimately to blame.

When I say no more, he clears his throat and then he fakes a smile as he states hesitantly, "I didn't realize. I mean when you said that you got rid of your parents, I thought it was an isolated incident. I had never thought that you would keep doing it. So, I guess I should ask just how many people have you killed?"

I knew that I should have never told him because now I have done it. I opened the Pandora's box and by the end of this he will be the death of me. All because I had to open my big damn mouth. After all, until now I have survived for one sole reason, because I had never let anyone live who knew or at least tried not to. And yet, he knows.

Now what should I do about it? Do I kill him too, even though I may love him. Or shall we play a little game?

As I tap my nails again on the door handle, a smirk plays on my lips, and I decide to go with the latter.

"Over the years, not including my parents......25." I say quietly while thinking that is a nice round number to start with.

"25? That sounds like you just pulled it out of your ass. Why don't you tell me the real truth?" He asks suggestively as he starts to laugh and mock me.

"What do you mean? I did tell you the honest to goodness truth." I reply quickly as I try to see where he is going with this.

He pauses while he raises his right hand and runs his thumb over the stubble on his chin. Then he states in a matter-of-fact tone of voice, "First of all, there is no goodness in this. There is just no place for it. We are talking about murdering people after all."

"Yes, that is true. However, I have not told you everything. See, I have another personality that takes over when things become too uncomfortable for me to deal with. It has happened ever since I was little. The first time was when my dad came in and showed me what he truly wanted of me." I say bitterly as I scoot down in my seat and glance out the window at the woods to the side.

When I hesitate, he reaches over and strokes my hand slowly with his. The warmth coaxes me on just enough to get out the rest of it before I stop and continue to stare. In the meantime, he says nothing, but I can tell he understands.

"Now, every time I hear the call of the kill, Joanna takes over and puts her face on to hunt for her next unsuspecting victim. The worst part is that to this day, I will never understand why I feel compelled to keep the earlobe as a souvenir. It's a strange feeling to need something close to you like that." I say absentmindedly as I lose my concentration and my voice trails off.

After a few minutes, I turn to see him moving around uncomfortably and then putting the car back into gear. For the moment he seems to be satisfied with what he has heard. I just hope that it doesn't come back to haunt me in the future.

By the time we end up stopping in the thickest part of the woods next to the lake, it is dark out and almost pitch black. It is overcast so the moon and stars are covered. That leaves very little for us to see by. So, he parks the car so the illumination from the brights, allows us to see what we are doing.

He gestures for me to walk over to him as he calls to me insistently while trying to get my attention, "Christy, come here."

I fake a smile as too many visions pop in my head of things I would do given this situation if it were on the opposite foot. Mainly, I would let him dispose of the body and then kill him off too before pushing him in. However, I don't see him doing this to me for some reason. Call it naïve, or maybe it is the fact that I can feel the pull between the two of us. Either way, I don't think he could harm me if he tried.

When I do reach his side, I notice something a bit off.

Chapter 6: What's Going On?

From the minute I look down in the water I feel the chill run up my spine as the cool breeze of the night air rushes past me. I know that this is a watery grave like no other. It is pitch black and the silt is so thick that I see a few dead fish floating just a few feet from us.

"Wow. What is the matter with this lake?" I ask curiously as the smell of dead fish suddenly hits me.

I pinch my nose with my right hand between my thumb and forefinger and curse under my breath, "Son-of-a-bitch."

When the stench almost forces me to start gagging, I step back a few feet towards the car before he says flatly while laughing at the look on my face, "It has gotten worse since I have been here last. The lake used to be so much better, but since I have been dumping my bodies here, it has declined steadily. I guess it has something to do with the fact that the beaver's built the damn."

I cock my head and ask quickly while gasping for air, "How many times have you come here? By the way, you never did answer my question and I think it is about time. So, fess up. How many people have you killed and why?"

He glances up at me with a glint in his eyes and then he looks away quickly. When he starts to open his mouth, I can already tell he is about to lie again by the way he squints and refuses to look me in the eyes as he replies quietly, "First of all, you need to know my past. When I was a child, my dad would beat the hell out of me. Almost to the point of death." He pauses before he goes on in a whisper, "As a matter of fact, I have a 3-inch scar behind my ear. It is under my hair right here."

As he says it, he points and parts the hair there so I can walk towards him and look. I lean in and see a long thin white line that stands out against the rest of his skin because of the stark difference in color.

"See." He states flatly before releasing the hair and turning to face me, "One time I woke up in my grandmother's arms after a particularly brutal beating. I had just made the mistake of walking in on my dad after a long day of work. With a beer in one hand and the remote in the other, he had looked up at me from his reclining chair and that is all it took. I was only 6 at the time, and my mother had already been dead for two years by then. Years later, just before my grandmother died, she begged for my forgiveness for not stopping him all those years. I think it took a little bit out of her every time she witnessed him beating me. I know that it screwed me up far more than I care to say."

This time when he stops speaking, there is a change in the air and the way he looks at me. For a moment, I see a man who I could love, the next all I see is hatred in his eyes as he demands flatly, "Help me get him in. No one will ever find him once the animals and fish have their way with him." He hesitates and sighs before adding in a softer tone of voice, "I am just sorry I didn't get their earlier."

He shakes his head and then between the two of us, we carry him over to the water's edge. Before we throw the body in, we swing it back and forth, so it goes out farther. After the lake absorbs the body, he turns away from me and mutters under his breath, "49."

Did he just say 49? I thought he had maybe killed one or two, but not 49. That rivals me. What the fuck? Who really is this man and what is he?

"Wait, did you just say 49?" I reply inquisitively as I stare at him and wrap my fingers around his wrist tightly to force him to look at me.

When he turns to look at me, he gazes deep into my eyes and then finally says slowly, "Yes. Why?"

"Because that means you are just like me, but better. I have been doing this for years, but it sounds like you have been doing this for decades." I state flatly as I keep eye contact with him.

His gaze stays unwavering as he replies before swallowing hard, "Yes, I suppose I have been. But that is neither here nor there. We need to get out of here before someone happens to just drive by or walk down the road. Occasionally, I do see some unlucky traveler while I am dumping a body and then I must get rid of them as well."

"Come on, let's get out of here." He says forcefully before he walks towards the car.

I cock my head and dare to yell after him as I begin to move in that direction, "Do you not keep a souvenir? I always do."

He stops in his tracks and then throws his head back to laugh wholeheartedly. When I reach him, he looks me dead in the eyes before stating matter-of-factly, "I only keep the index finger of my intended victim. This man was just in my way and threatening our bond."

Have I just found the man of my dreams? Or a nightmare in disguise? For if he can kill someone so easily like I can, what if he gets sick of me and decides I am threatening his lifestyle? Of course, to say the least, what if I decide that I am done with him? Will I kill him or just disappear into the night?

I think about this on the way back to my apartment and find myself wondering if we can really make this work between two serial killers.

Chapter 7: Do As I Say

As I stare into his handsome greenish blue eyes, I keep wondering about our fate. "How will this all work out if we both have insatiable appetites?" I think to myself as he opens the door for me to the apartment complex.

Nick spots me before he realizes that there is a man with me.

"Hey gorgeous. I was thinking that tonight might be the night?" he asks smoothly as he watches Jon walk up next to me and stop.

Of course, Jon is a good foot taller than he is, so he finds himself forced to look up at him before returning his gaze to me. "Oh, sorry man. I didn't know you were there." He says before running his fingers through his long blonde hair and wincing.

He acts like he is ready to get punched in the nose. However, when Jon doesn't hit him, he smiles brightly and waves before saying, "I will be going now. Talk to you later Joanna."

"What did he just say?" I think to myself in a panic as I look between Nick and Jon while just hoping that he didn't hear it.

After all, this whole time I led Jon to believe that my name really is Christy. How could I have been so foolish to think that the charade could go on forever? Not to mention, the moment he ended up back here and I found out that he may be sticking around for a while, I should have told him the truth.

"Shit!" I murmur under my breath before sighing and facing the music.

When I look into his eyes this time, that glint is back, and he is smirking like someone who knows something they shouldn't. And when he states flatly, "We should head inside because people are staring." I just stand there for a few seconds stupidly.

"Joanna, we really should go in. Your neighbors seem to be getting an eyeful." He says quietly while leading me to my front door by the elbow.

"Where are your keys?" he whispers after someone walks up behind us.

While not even bothering to look back, I reply quietly as I pull them out of my purse and dangle them in front of his face, "Sorry, this all has just been too much for me today. Here you go."

He snatches them from me quickly and then unlocks the door before opening it. Just as soon as we are safely inside and the door is shut behind us, I feel a strange sense of easiness around him that I have never felt before with anyone. I look up into his eyes and feel so much more than I can express in words.

The closest I can come is gratitude, love, or this immense overpowering feeling of belonging. I believe that is the word. Belonging. I belong to him.

Once the strange silence is broken when he demands authoritatively, "Bedroom now." I feel much better about this whole thing.

Even though I still have so many questions that need answers, I can deal with the way things are now just fine because he is here with me. So, I head towards the bedroom with a smile because I have the feeling that he is about to make everything better. Matter of fact, I know he will.

After I step inside the dark bedroom suite, I turn on the light and immediately glance down at the swelling in his pants. A smirk forms in the corners of my mouth before I flick out my tongue hungrily. Even though I have had a day full of sexual depravity, I crave more because it is from him.

He points at my clothes with a stern look on his face as he demands in urgency, "Take them off now.

As I slowly obey, I watch him slip his pants down and his rock-hard cock stand at attention. Then he picks them up quickly before throwing them over the back of the black faux suede chair in the corner. After he does this, he walks over to me and points to the ground in front of him, before declaring, "You will get down on your knees and wrap those pretty little lips around my cock. I want to feel you suck me like you mean it."

The last thing I expect is for him to guide me down as he wraps his fingers in the hair on the back of my head. With his other hand he rubs his thumb over my lower lip and then forces me to open as he slips his thumb in. I lick it and suck right before I bite down playfully on it.

When he gazes into my eyes, I can tell that he sees the playful intent as he smirks and then replaces his thumb with his cock. As he runs the tip slowly over my lips before thrusting it in, I see something else in his eyes. Could that be admiration or love? Or am I mistaken?

Can two serial killers actually love each other? I bet Sigmund Freud had never thought about that one before. Especially, when most of the time all he seemed to care about is if you had daddy issues or worshipped your mother.

"That's a good girl. I love the way you feel in my hands. But what I love more is when you are wrapped around him." As he says it in a husky voice, he guides him in between my lips forcefully before sliding him down my throat.

I surely don't think it can go any further, but he proves me wrong when he fills me to the hilt.

"Oh baby, your mouth fills so warm and tight." He says breathlessly while starting to thrust him in and out.

I feel Joanna struggling to surface, but I push her back down finally before I reach up and wrap my fingers around his balls tightly as I squeeze with one hand. My left-hand scraps my nails up the inner thigh of his leg slowly and stops just below his ass. Then he moans uncontrollably as his leg begins to shake.

"Fuck! Baby you feel so good." He whispers while he tightens his fist in my hair and forces me closer.

When I feel his cock thicken and his balls harden, I know that he is about to burst. I welcome it and wait for the warmth as I stare up into his half-hooded eyes, filled with pleasure. He moans and then yells, "I am coming." Before he jerks and the hot liquid shoots down my throat. As it spurts and coats my tongue as well, I close my eyes and revel in the knowledge that he feels so good because of what I have done.

Chapter 8: What Is This?

After he helps me up carefully, I sit on the edge of the bed and watch as he thoughtfully wipes the remaining seed off my lips. When he is finished, he takes my hand and leads me up to the head of the bed. He looks down at me and smiles mischievously as I climb on the silky sheets and feel the heat of his gaze on my ass as I move.

Oh, how I love it when he hungers for me so. Honestly, I didn't think I would ever find a man that would make me feel anything, let alone this heart pounding, gut wrenching feeling that I like to think is love. After all, I have never experienced love in my life, so how would I know what it feels like?

"Baby, where does it hurt?" he asks thoughtfully as he surveys my cuts and bruises.

"Here and here, and there." I reply in almost a whisper as I slowly point to the general direction of my ribs, my bruised folds, and the sensitive skin between my legs.

He shakes his head before stating sadly, "He must have done one hell of a job on you. I am just sorry that I didn't get there earlier."

When I look up into his eyes, I see a strangeness there. What is this? Is this the look of a man in love? I could have sworn that I saw it earlier in his eyes, but this time it is unmistakable. Or is it pity? If it is, I could never stay with him.

"Yeah, he did. As far as I can tell, he knocked me out and then tied me up before doing whatever he wanted to do to me. I guess I am just lucky that I can't get pregnant. I murmur under my breath as I wince when he runs his fingers gently over my ribs.

"I will never let this happen again. From now on you will stay by my side. No other man will ever touch you again." he says in a domineering voice.

I must squash it quickly though, because my killer instinct will win eventually and that means I must be with other men. Even if it is only for a few minutes so I can kill them afterwards and quench my thirst for blood for the time being. So, as I look up into his handsome eyes, I swallow hard and clear my throat to say softly, "Actually, at some point I am going to need to have sex with other men because that is how I get my prey and I have been doing this for far too long to stop now. I need it."

"Not if I can help it, you won't." He remarks quietly as he brushes my inner thigh just barely with the palm of his hand.

I cock my head and look at him inquisitively before I ask, "So, how do you plan on stopping me? This is who I am. Why would you want to? And why do you care so much in the first place?"

As he reaches for the drawer, a smirk plays on his lips, and he stops for a moment in thought. When he continues what he is doing, he doesn't say a word. Instead, he pulls out the leather straps and then shuts the drawer. The look on his face changes to one of a man who is on a mission as he opens his mouth slowly and replies flatly, "I will keep you tied up if I must. You are mine and no other. Do you hear me?" he declares and then asks angrily.

"Now, for the time being I would rather show you how gentle a man can be." He whispers when I don't reply.

The moment he straps me down, my body becomes hypersensitive. I feel a real sense of urgency in him, but he pushes it back for my sake. I know that he really wants to nail me good and hard but after the other man got down with me, I am broken and worn. It is a wonder that he even wants me anymore after that.

A few minutes later, he disappears into the bathroom, and I hear the water running. I wonder what on earth he is up to until he comes back out with a towel and a wash rag. Ah, I think he is about to clean me up.

When he walks over to me with a serious look in his eyes, I watch him sit on the edge of the bed as he leans over me and runs the washrag carefully over my face.

At first, he traces the lines of my bleeding lips before he wipes my forehead and then my cheeks. After he is finished, he moves down to the rest of me. When he brushes my inner thighs with the rag, I shutter because it is so sensitive that it hurts a little.

"Does that even hurt?" he asks lovingly with a worried look on his face.

I nod, and then lick my lips before answering slowly, "Yeah. He really did a number on me. I don't know all that he did while I was out, but I can guess by where my body hurts."

"If that son of a bitch wasn't already dead, I would have had to go hunt him down and make him feel it in the worst way. I think I would have sodomized him with something sharp and made him bleed internally before I cut off his dick and fed it to him. Show him exactly how it feels for once. That is right before I disemboweled him and then slit his throat. He would be gasping for air while his manhood was in his mouth." He says angrily as he clenches his fists and glares at the wall.

"It would be the last time he ever did that to anyone." he adds as he glances down at me with pain in his eyes.

I briefly forget that I am tied up, so I go to reach up to touch his face and find that I must stop. He glances up at the cuffs and smiles before he finishes what he started by gingerly rubbing my swollen folds. As he parts them, his lips open and I hear him begin to breathe raggedly. I know that he needs me now and I can prove it.

As I look up into his eyes, I lick my lips again slowly and then beg in a sweet voice, "Please, please I need you to fill me now. I need to feel you deep inside me, so it replaces the pain."

He hesitates but then removes the rag and stands up before placing it on the end table and grabbing my play toy. When he returns, he has a big smile on his face, but his eyes are hooded and full of desire. As he turns it on, my slit begins to pulsate in anticipation.

"Please." I coo as I wiggle in delight.

I need it in me right now and nothing else matters.

Chapter 9: To Be Desired

When the tip of it presses against my nub, I shutter and automatically clench my folds together. I cry out in need, "Please." before he applies more pressure and slowly traces the slit of my folds with his index finger carefully.

After teasing me for a moment, he inserts his middle finger an inch and then runs it around in a circle. It tickles as he keeps playing with me until I beg more insistently, "Oh, please. Please I will do anything."

"Mm. That's what I was waiting to hear. Of course, you will let me do anything to you anyways because you can't help it." He replies while a Cheshire cat smile plays on his lips.

The glint in his eyes returns as he rubs the vibrator over my clit and slides in another finger. When he slips in a third, I begin to moan and pant. However, when he starts to slide in the fourth, I feel my lips strain and stretch. It hurts but I say nothing because the pleasure of it all has already almost brought me to the edge.

As he runs the vibrator down to my rim and then hesitates, I scream, "I am almost there. Don't stop now."

I need to be filled in both, and I am ready to explode. So, I stare into his eyes and plead with him, "Please, please, please." when he stays still and just stares at me with a big grin on that damn handsome face of his.

"Fuck you." I scream at him finally when being sweet doesn't achieve the needed response.

His eyes widen and he throws his head back before laughing loudly. "Oh, is that how it is now?" he says playfully before he withdraws the vibrator and his fingers.

He raises his fingers to his mouth and licks them clean as he watches for the way I respond. As he does it, I close my eyes and wiggle around while bucking up and down and trying to rub my thighs together to relieve the need deep inside.

The moment I stop and look up at him, I notice that he is staring at me intently. I swallow hard and then beg one last time pitifully, "Please."

It is at that moment he decides to climb between my legs and leans down to slowly kiss my inner thighs. As he works his way up to my soaked folds, he takes his time and kisses every inch of silky skin. When he reaches my nub, he flicks it with his tongue before he devours it hungrily as if it was a piece of candy.

He sucks on it as his fingers find my entrances and simultaneously penetrates them. I moan loudly and arch my back as he sucks harder and begins to work his magic. "Fuck!" I exclaim loudly when he bites down and slides another finger in.

While twirling his fingers in a circle, he begins to lick my nub and brings me right to the edge before he stops again. This time when he withdraws, he replaces it with the tip of his throbbing cock. The precum glistens in the moonlight because by now the clouds have cleared and the full moon is shining bright through the bedroom window.

I arch my back even more, so he hits my spot when he thrusts in, and I find myself wishing that he hadn't tied me so tight. Right now, I would have loved to wrap my fingers in his hair and dig my nails into his back, but I can't. Especially when he fills me to his balls and then holds it there for a few seconds. He looks down at me and whispers, "Are you alright?"

I nod, and smile before he begins to thrust in and out steadily. While wishing that he would hurry, I am glad in a way that he is going slowly because I can already feel the pain coming back to me. As it does, the memories come flooding in from earlier today when I woke up and he was on top of me.

When I wince, he sees it and stops. He gazes down at me lovingly and asks again softly, "Baby, am I hurting you?"

I shake my head as I reply in a whisper hoarsely, "No. I was just remembering earlier. Sorry."

He stops and thinks for a moment as I feel him throb deep inside of me. As his shaft pulsates, I clench around him and then assure him that it is alright by stating sweetly, "It's O.K. Matter of fact, it is better than O.K. because I think I love you."

The moment I say it, I can't believe my ears. "What the hell did I just say?" I ask myself as I gaze up into his eyes and see the shock in them.

Shit, shit, shit. By the way he is staring at me, he does not feel the same way. But I thought for sure he did because he is taking such good care of me. How could I have been so wrong about something that feels so right? More importantly, how could I have been so stupid to blurt out something so important like this?

After hesitating, that strange look returns to his eyes and he glances away for a moment before he gazes at me and says sincerely, "Joanna, I have come to realize that I love you too. I don't really know how this happened, but I guess it has nipped us both in the butt. Now, the question is what to do about it? I for one, am going to make you cum so hard that you won't ever need to fuck another man again. Even if it is so you can kill him. There simply must be another way."

When he leans down to devour my mouth before I get to say another word, I clench tightly around him and then eagerly await his response. As he begins to thrust in and out again, I moan into his mouth before he breaks the kiss and then straights up so he can begin to pound even harder now. Forget about soft and sweet, right now I need him, and I mean all of him as hard as he can give it.

"Fuck me harder." I yell as I arch my back to meet him halfway.

As my insides pulsate, I feel his cock throb more and more as the pressure builds and he finally thrusts one last time before he yells, "I can't hold it anymore."

As he fills me, I let go and finally feel my release when my body begins to shake uncontrollably, and I bite my lower lip. I shut my eyes and see one of the most beautiful lightshows that I have ever seen unfold beneath a wonderous sky. No wonder, why people that are truly in love are always happy. Surely, they must have sex like this all the time.

It is a minute later when I realize that he has collapsed on top of me, and he has no control. I hear him sigh and breath heavily on top of me before he finally musters enough strength to push up and kiss me sweetly before straightening to look at me from above. He smiles down at me with love in his eyes. Yes, love.

"Baby, you bring out the animal in me. Now, let's get these off so we can clean up. But don't you go running off on me again." He says jokingly as he undoes them and then climbs off the bed.

I watch as he walks to the bathroom, and I sit up on the edge of the bed. All the while I can't help but think how lucky I am to have him.

Chapter 10: What Do I Do Now?

After we both use the bathroom and clean up, I slip under the silk sheets, and he slides in behind me. I hear him snore softly about five minutes later as I struggle to sleep. Damn it all. That man was supposed to have been my precious prey, but now all I can think about is when and where I will find the next one once Jon becomes preoccupied with his job.

So far, he has managed to spend time with me, but what happens the moment he must go back to work? I know what. I will end up slipping out and meeting Mr. Right For That Moment and fucking his brains out before slitting his throat. I need to feel the warmth of the blood as it pumps from his veins, while I watch the life drain from his face slowly. Then I take his earlobe to add to my collection for later when I want to remember the feeling of the kill.

I squirm in bed as my slit becomes wet with desire because I need it as much as I need to breathe. When I can't take it anymore, I slide my hand down to my clit and pinch it before I slip my other hand between my legs. As soon as I feel the heat, I penetrate my slippery lips with two fingers to satisfy the ache. Round and round my fingers go, as they twist and turn while I rub my nub voraciously because I need to feel alive again.

A moan escapes my lips softly and I quickly stop to look over to see if Jon hears it. When he doesn't move, I smirk and then close my eyes as I slip a third finger in and the throbbing between my legs becomes a storm. As my fingers slip around in my juices and start to make a loud sucking sound, I feel him turn over and face the other way.

I tense for a moment as I stop and listen for his snoring. Finally, after a few seconds I hear the soft sounds coming from him and I begin to rub my clit more forcefully now. I can't handle it anymore, so I bite down on my lower lip and then I feel it rip right through me as I jerk on the bed unintentionally.

He turns over and suddenly sits up while I clench my fingers and continue to rub through it all. I moan and then he realizes exactly what I am doing. He smirks and then lays down and snuggles up behind me before I feel his shaft become hard against my ass.

When he rubs the tip against my rim a few minutes later, I sigh and then he replaces it with his wet finger to tease me. I smile secretively because I love it when he fills me rear. Hell, I love it when he shoves his cock in all my entrances. Now if he just had three of them, I would be in heaven.

While feeling his finger slip in and out, I begin to rub my nub again, slowly this time because there is no rush. Then he begins kissing the back of my neck and a shiver runs up and down my spine before he thrusts his cock all the way in and stops. I feel it throb and then the veins begin to pulsate as he stays still for a minute longer and licks my earlobe.

"That's the spot. Right there." I think to myself as he begins to thrust in and out as his fingers dig into my hip.

As I keep rubbing, I tighten my ring around him and he whispers in my ear, "Baby, you are so fucking tight tonight. When I woke up and found you fingering yourself, I just couldn't help it. After all, I love filling all of you."

He slows down and we begin a delicate dance as our two bodies push and pull against each other. As I shove my ass harder into him, he thrusts deeper and deeper into me, and I feel as if I am about to scream. I do suddenly and then he quickly stops and turns me over before he spreads my legs and climbs between them. While staring down at me, he whispers seriously, "Joanna, I love you. I want to shout it to the world, so everyone hears. But I also know that this is a tricky situation."

I reach up and wrap my fingers around the back of his neck before replying quickly, "Oh, I don't care right now. I just need you to shut up and fuck me."

Realizing that it sounded a bit callous, I smile while adding softly, "I'm joking. Now, just shut up and kiss me."

He laughs and then plants his hands firmly on my hips before digging his fingers in and thrusting as hard as he can.

There. Now that is what I am talking about.

I smile and that is all the answer he needs as he fills me harder and harder while I feel myself slip further away. Joanna is taking over, and I can't do a damn thing. Unfortunately, I watch from the sidelines in a drunken haze while seeing bits and pieces of their love fest all night long. They try every position imaginable, and they never get tired of each other. When they finally collapse on the bed at 6 a.m., I cry out and she lets me through.

By this time, I hate myself even more. That should have been me, not her. Yet, all I could do was to hide in the corner and see bits and pieces like a kid at an 18 plus carnival show. Why on earth?

"Wait, I think I know. Either she thinks she is protecting my heart, or she is in love with him also. If she loves him, how do I get rid of her for good so I can have my happy ending with him?" I think to myself as I suddenly remember that she can read my thoughts and she already knows what I am planning to do.

Chapter 11: The Consequences Of His Actions

For some reason I already knew what had to happen when I woke up in her arms and heard my phone ringing.

"Baby, that was my boss. You know the drill. This time maybe you will listen to me and not decide to go fuck someone else. After all, must I remind you of what happened yesterday? Maybe, when I get back, we can find a way for you to still do your thing without fucking them." I say as I slip my shoes on quickly and make sure my wallet is still in my pocket.

She rolls her eyes because we both know that isn't going to happen if her other has her way. So, as I watch her hunch her shoulders and then say while sounding resigned, "I will try but I can't guarantee what she will decide to do after you leave.

After all, as it seems she is getting more and more control over me, even if I am trying to keep it at bay."

I gaze at her for a long time and then shake my head in frustration. "I knew that this would be problematic, but dealing with two women is just too much. You need to get her under control. That is all I am going to say because I must go. Now really, stay put!" I exclaim as I walk towards the door because I need to hurry before he calls back or sends someone to look for me.

By the time I walk in the door to the captain's office, it is too late because my phone is buzzing in my pocket. When he looks up at me quickly, he smiles and then puts the phone down before stating sarcastically, "Ah, you finally made it. What a pleasure to see you. I guess you finally decided to grace us with your presence."

I stop where I stand and open my mouth to speak but before I get to reply, he asks, "By any chance did you happen to find out where she is dumping the bodies yet?"

I decide that this is a conversation for a later date, so I take a seat in front of his desk and feel the cold steel radiating through my grey dress pants. They must have the air conditioning on because there is a chill in the air, and it is 80 degrees outside.

"Well?" he asks inquisitively as he taps his fingers on the desk like a drum several times.

While swallowing hard, I scan the room and find nothing of importance. So, I return my gaze to the captain before answering slowly, "Well, what?"

"Don't play stupid with me. You know full well what. Now tell me. Or have you forgotten that this is a job because you are too busy filling her holes?"

"Alright. Cut it out. No, I haven't. I am getting to the point that I am beginning to really wonder if she is really a serial killer in the first place. All I have seen is one beautiful woman who desperately just wants to fit in and feel love." I state flatly as I look out the window.

I hear the captain clear his throat before he whispers so no one outside the door can hear, "Do you love her? Please don't tell me you do. After all, there are rules and regulations in place because of situations like this one. You are too good of a detective for this."

"Of course not. How could I? The relationship has been built on lies. I don't even know her real name, but I do know that it is not Joanna. I checked into her background, and she doesn't exist before her teenage years. All that I do know is that she is hiding from something and that she was molested as a child. Perhaps she is running from someone." I say matter-of-factly as I stare him in the eyes.

"Well find out. I need to know before the next man is killed or ends up disappearing. I am worried about you Jon. You are a good man, but you often forget that you are a detective and what your job is. Now, go back and find out for me where those bodies are and exactly who she is running from." He says sternly while furrowing his brow.

I know I am in over my head, and I can't go back now, but I can't turn away from her because she means more to me than anyone else on this earth. After all, we are the same and are two peas in a pod.

"Alright. I will. But don't keep calling me. One of these times she is going to pick up the phone and find out who I really am. This all would be over for nothing." I reply quietly while I stand and look out the door.

I watch as the room becomes eerily quiet, then suddenly they all seem to start talking at once after I reach for the door and open it.

"Don't forget. Get me that info pronto. It is imperative to the case Jon." He yells after me as I walk out and glare at each of them.

"Someone must have been gossiping and now I am the talk of the town apparently. Oh well. At least I have the most gorgeous woman in the whole world in my bed at night." I think to myself as I smile and casually walk out the front door.

As I look up at the bright sky, I wonder if Joanna is still there or if she has decided that she just had an itch that must be scratched. Then I drive back in hopes that

I am wrong about her and that she will be waiting open armed with a smile and a kiss. On the way there, I start to feel as if I am in a dream, and this has all happened once before.

Eventually, as I keep driving, all the cars merge into one as I stare ahead at the road, but I notice something when I look in the review mirror. I no longer look like the haunted man I once was with disheveled hair, a scraggly beard and blank eyes that stare into nothingness. Before me sits a man with a future that contains someone special. I had never thought that possible, especially with my past time.

When I had killed my first victim, I would have never imagined that I could love someone, and they would love me in return. But here I am, a man in love with the most beautiful woman in the world, and the possibilities are endless.

Chapter 12: How Strong?

I sat there for hours and fought to keep control as Joanna kept begging to come out and play. She wanted to go looking for another man to kill, but I refused and that seemed to make her even more angry. However, I used my love for Jon to fight back and stay, so he knows that I meant what I said.

When I hear the door open and he walks in before stopping with a shocked look on his face, I can already tell that he is so surprised that I am standing here staring at him.

"You stayed for me?" he asks hesitantly while crossing the distance between us.

He looks down at me lovingly and smiles before he wraps his hands around my waist and picks me up. Then he devours my mouth while staring into my soul. He knows that he owns me now just as long as Joanna stays where she belongs. Especially, when I wrap my legs around him and refuse to let go. So, he slams me against the wall while one hand moves up to my breast and the other moves to my mouth.

He runs his thumb softly over my lips as I nip and suck at it before he traces the line of my jaw to the back of my neck. Then he curls his fingers in my hair and forces my face upwards. Now I am directly staring into his eyes as I feel him become rock-hard against my slit and he growls. There is something different about him, I can already feel it even though he has just returned.

When he devours my mouth again feverishly as he holds my head still, my hands run up and down his back before I manage to pull his shirt out of his pants. I slide my hands under it and feel the warmth of his skin on my palms. Oh, it feels so good the way his body reacts with mine and is in tune with every movement I make.

"Fuck. You taste so good!" he exclaims as he hungrily bites at my lips while not wasting any time to find a place to put me for a minute.

As he sits me down on the entry way table, he quickly runs his hands up under my red and green plaid miniskirt before he rips off my lacey dark green panties with one swift movement.

"God damn it!" he cries out when he lifts the miniskirt and sees that my bruises are darker than they were earlier.

While furrowing his brow, he asks with concern on his face as he gently traces the outlines of them, "Do they hurt?"

"Not much. But when you touch me, it makes it all better." I reply quietly because there could be someone just outside the door.

The apartment walls are quite thin, so I always make sure to try and keep it down. Especially, when the likes of Nick are running around. After all, I don't want to give him the wrong ideas about me.

"Alright but tell me if it hurts too much. I love giving you pleasure through pain, but this is just not right." He states sadly while his finger finds my soaked folds and begins to rub it up and down along the slit.

I throw my head back and close my eyes as he continues before he picks me up and carries me to the couch.
"That's better I think." He remarks as he nestles his upper body between my legs.

It is at this exact moment when I become inspired and say seductively, "I have an idea, but I need something out of my purse first."

He looks up at me with a smirk on his lips and says softly, "Alright, I will bite. What?"

"Just you never mind. Let me up for a minute and you will see." I say mischievously as my leg skips over his head and then I sit up.

When I stand, I find where I dropped my purse the moment we came in and then I rifle through it until I find my skinning knife that is razor sharp and cuts anything like it is butter in the very bottom. As I turn around with the knife against my lips, I smile wickedly before I step towards him.

He takes one look at it and stands up quickly, then his eyes come back up to mine as I see anger in him.

"Just calm down. I would never hurt you, but I do like to play." I purr quietly as I watch him relax a little bit and sit back down.

"Mind you, we both like our knives, but usually when someone takes one out it means they intend on harming me." He says softly while he tries to play it off as nothing, but I know better.

"So, what do you plan on doing with that?" he asks hesitantly as his eyes track my every movement now like a lion watching its prey before it strikes.

"Wait and see. Now come here." I say quietly to calm his inner beast as I hold out my left hand and beckon for him to walk to me.

There is something to say when the only thing that lets you feel alive is when you slice your skin open with cold steel and watch as your warm blood pours out of your body. I remember a long time ago when I was little, my uncle told me lovingly as I snuggled in his arms, "Life is so fragile, one slice of a knife can end your whole world."

Years later, after I had killed 17 men, I sat down and remembered what he had said. At first, it didn't fully hit me what he meant by it. Not until I accidentally slit my own skin and watched the crimson blood as it leaked down my arm and stained my white jeans.

Chapter 13: The Thrill Of Desire

"Seriously, come here." I say seductively as I watch his eyes become bigger and bigger.

I don't think he realizes that I am serious about this, until I close the gap between us and stare up into his eyes. Then and only then, he swallows hard and says hesitantly while sounding a little unsure of himself, "Now what?"

I giggle because I get to do something new with him that he has never experienced before like this. When I look into his eyes, I feel giddy before running the tip of my knife up the exposed skin of his inner arm. It leaves a little trail of blood as I make a small cut about 6 inches long. Not deep enough to cause harm, but definitely something he feels.

"What are you doing?" he asks me curiously as he furrows his brow.

I don't say a word as I lean down and lick it with my tongue. Then I reach up with my other hand and force him to meet me halfway as I kiss him. He licks my lips and growls hungrily. I think to myself "he got the point" as his eyes light up and he grabs my wrist tightly.

He growls again while his eyes ask for more and he states in a husky voice, "Baby, I want you so bad right now. This is so kinky, but I want to fuck you while we do it to each other."

"Mhm." I smile as I agree with him because I have never experienced this with someone I cared about as I feel Joanna trying to come out.

"One time I played with my prey and fucked him like an animal as we took turns cutting each other." I blurt out while not thinking about it.

"Did I really say that?" I murmur under my breath as I shrug my shoulders and then stare at him to see what he thinks.

He looks up at me in confusion before he laughs it off and states sarcastically, "I guess he got his just desserts, didn't he?"

I hesitate and then reply quietly, "Yes, he did."

What I didn't tell him was that this one man in particular, I had chosen to keep around for a while before Joanna got a wild hair up her butt and slit him from ear to ear while we were playing a game of cat and mouse.

He laughs nervously because he is probably wondering when Joanna will come out to play and slit his throat while he sleeps. Of course, I would never let that happen if I could help it. And I often wonder if she doesn't love him as much as I do, so it probably isn't even an issue.

When I realize that the conversation has gotten too serious and we have lost the moment, I wrap my fingers around his wrist and pull him to me before standing on my tip toes and kissing him hungrily. Then after we come up for air, I whisper sweetly, "I am sorry that I ruined the mood."

He fakes a smile and then replies sarcastically, "Baby, I could never be truly mad at you. Just let me fuck you and I will forgive you."

A smirk spreads across my lips as he picks me back up. This time, I don't intend on stopping him for nothing as he carries me to the couch and releases me. My body bounces off the soft cushion as I watch him strip down and then descend upon me with a raging hard on. At first, he nestles in between my knees with his mouth just above my soaked folds. I close my eyes when I feel his breath on my nub and the flat of his tongue.

But a moment later, I squeal in delight as his nose rubs my clit and the tip of his tongue moves down my slit before sliding in. It is an interesting feeling for someone who has never experienced it before because Joanna didn't think it was good to feel so vulnerable in the arms of someone who you are about to kill.

When I start to hold my breath, he stops and looks up at me curiously before asking seriously, "Does it not feel good?"

I shake my head furiously because I gave him completely the wrong idea. When I realize this, I reach down to touch his face gently and sit up before replying sadly with big puppy dog eyes, "Oh, no. It feels wonderful. I just have never had a guy go down on me before."

After I gaze at him with so much love, I whisper, "I loved it, but I want something else right now."

He smirks as he lowers his hand to rub the tip of his cock where the precum is glistening. As I watch him, I slit a small cut into my lower arm and at the same time, I feel his tip slide into my lips.

"Mm." I hear him moan as he throws his head back and I raise the knife up to his throat.

Immediately, I start to lose control as Joanna tries to force her way in like a tornado. I step back quickly and shake my head while my vision blurs. "No!" I exclaim while fighting with her.

I feel him grab me by the wrist, but I can't see him as she continues to try and take over. "No." I cry out before he releases me and takes a few steps back himself.

He is confused, I can tell by the way he looks at me with doubt in his eyes. Supposedly, he loves me, but we will soon see when he finds out that Joanna is my stronger half.

"Baby, what's wrong?" he asks softly as he places a hand on my shoulder.

He pulls me to his chest and envelopes me in his strong arms. Suddenly, I am surrounded by all his manly scent, and it is intoxicating as hell. I close my eyes and lean into his body as I feel Joanna go bye-bye for now. As I smile, and relish the fact that he loves me, I let him keep me warm and slowly chip away at the wall that is me.

When I don't say anything for a while, I feel him release me and put me at arm's length before he asks with concern in his eyes, "Joanna, what happened?"

At first, I doubt if he even fully understands that I really do have a split personality, because he acts as if he can't comprehend what I am going through. Especially, when I sit him down a few minutes later and explain it to him point blank what is going on. Then suddenly he looks up at me after several minutes of a blank expression and asks thoughtfully, "So, what happens if she takes over and refuses to ever relinquish control again. I mean, if she is stronger than you, how would you fight back and regain control?"

"Honestly, that is the problem, isn't it?" I murmur under my breath as I fight back the tears when I fully realize that my personality would be lost in time, plain and simple.

I would exist no more.

    The End of Part Two Love Me Now.

To my loving husband, mom, sister and all my family that believed in me enough to push me to make this all possible. Thank you. I love you all.

I also want to extend my deepest gratitude to all those who have read my books and to those who review them. Without your help, they would go unnoticed. Thank you all.

M.D. LaBelle

About the Author

M.D. LaBelle is an international award-winning, bestselling author. Her genres include anything from children's books to Erotica. She lives in Michigan with her loving husband and four of the six children. Most recently she has started writing on over 200 paid web novel platforms and her 38 books are on all online bookstores. Please, feel free to visit her website, Instagram, Twitter and Facebook. Visit M.D. LaBelle's website at

www.mdlabelle.com

Instagram Account

www.instagram.com/M.D.LaBelle/

Twitter Account

www.twitter.com/MDLaBelle1

Facebook Account

www.facebook.com/profile.php?id=100062142582314

I hope you enjoyed reading Part Two of The Bad Behavior Series Love Me Now. Please take the time to read all my other novels if you haven't already. Thank you.

Review it. Please review this novel and let others know what you liked about this book. If you write a review, please send an email to me at m.d.labelle0@gmail.com. Or if you want, please visit me at www.mdlabelle.com

Love Me Now

Part Two Of The Bad Behavior Series

Copyright © 2023 M.D. LaBelle

Casper Publishing

All Rights Reserved

This book is a work of fiction. Characters and names are of the author's imagination or are used fictitiously. Any resemblance to an actual person, living or dead, is entirely coincidental.

All rights are reserved. No part of this publication may be reproduced, distributed, or transmitted in any form or by any means, including photocopying, recording, or other electronic or mechanical methods, without the express prior written permission of the publisher, except in the case of brief quotations embodied in critical reviews and certain other noncommercial uses permitted by copyright law. For permission requests, please contact the author through her website: www.mdlabelle.com

www.ingramcontent.com/pod-product-compliance
Lightning Source LLC
LaVergne TN
LVHW012029060526
838201LV00061B/4520